THE TALE OF
ALBERT WALKER

Historical Fiction Depicting Village Life In Jamaica
1860s to 1930s

Garfield O. Heron Manderson

LMH PUBLISHING LIMITED

Work Cited
(Chapter 2: Maas Albert Became Ill)

Thompson, Eulalee. "Jamaica 1851 Cholera Outbreak." *Sunday Gleaner*. Kingston: The Gleaner Company Limited, 2010. 11-3. Print.

Editor: K. Sean Harris
Book Design, Layout & Typesetting: Roshane Mullings

Published by LMH Publishing Limited
Suite 10-11, Sagicor Industrial Park
7 Norman Road
Kingston C.S.O., Jamaica
Tel.: 876-938-0005; 876-938-0712
Fax: 876-759-8752
Email: lmhbookpublishing@cwjamaica.com
Website: www.lmhpublishing.com

Printed in the U.S.A.   ISBN: 978-976-8245-75-5

NATIONAL LIBRARY OF JAMAICA CATALOGUING-IN-PUBLICATION DATA

Manderson, Garfield O. Heron
    The tale of Albert Walker : historical fiction depicting village life in
Jamaica 1860s to 1930s / Garfield O. Heron Manderson.

    p. : ill. ; cm
ISBN 978-976-8245-75-5 (pbk).

1. Historical fiction   2. Jamaica – History – Fiction
3. Jamaica – Social life and customs – Fiction
I. Title

808.8381   dc 23

DEDICATION

My late grandfather Leslie Manderson, daughter Mehalia Manderson, my wife Ann Marie and to all Jamaican youth.

It is my hope that this historical novel will promote an appetite for reading and learning more of Jamaica's culture among our youth.

FOREWORD

Jamaica's culture and history are gradually being eroded by a plethora of postmodern ideals. The Tale of Albert Walker gives the young reader (as well as adults) a basic knowledge of what Jamaica was like in the late eighteen hundreds into the early nineteenth century. This book will give the reader an appreciation for Jamaica's culture and history.

CONTENTS

Introduction

Village Life in Jamaica 1862 to early 1930s

The year was 1862. Jamaica was emancipated some twenty-four years ago from slavery. While the former slaves relished their freedom and refused to go back to the plantations even under the then apprenticeship program, it resulted in an almost complete downturn of the Jamaican economy.

It was true that slavery was abolished but the lack of employment for some 200,000 or more of the island's population resulted in another form of slavery: idleness and uncontrolled drinking. Loitering on the streets of Kingston and the capital Spanish Town was also a constant problem.

Daily there were hundreds of men who were constantly on the lookout for work. Some found work at the harbour in Kingston, others became seasoned fishermen and many were employed on the new railroads which plied Kingston to Spanish Town and later expanded to other parts of the island.

Those who were educated or could be educated were recruited for the militia, and there were those employed to work in and around the barracks. Others were hired to work at the post office, the hospitals and schools.

These jobs were regarded as very important although it was rumored that the average black Jamaican man was not paid half the amount as his white counterpart.

There were some however, who went back to the plantations to work. The reason for this was that when the plantation owners could not get sufficient labour for their farms, they imported indentured labourers from India, Pakistan and even China. These indentured labourers generally prospered in Jamaica and although they were not paid very much, made the best of their situation. The average black man perceived that these Indians were doing well and so out of the perception that indentured labourers were well paid, they went back to the cane fields, only to discover that indentured labourers were paid low wages and that they would have to settle for the same.

Most ordinary Jamaicans however, took their families and went to live in the rural areas. From these rural migrations sprang some of the most organized villages and communities. Among some of these villages were Sligoville in St. Catherine, Gordon Town in St. Andrew and Highgate in St. Mary.

There were other deep rural communities such as Mavis Bank on the borders of St. Andrew and St. Thomas. Jacks Hill was another of these villages, so too were Hermitage and Golden Spring. These villages were outlined similar to the British medieval villages, where village life revolved around the church. Each of these villages had a church and a school, with houses either linear, meaning along the road leading to the village square or central, where the road led to the village and houses surrounded the main square.

Villagers would attend church on Sundays where the Anglican bishop or priest would officiate. The villagers had great respect for their parson and would address him as Father or Reverend. Church would begin at nine o'clock on Sunday mornings, ending the latest two o'clock in the afternoon.

Most village squares had a shop and bar where basic food items were sold. Villagers would buy salt fish, flour, cornmeal, shad, salt mackerel or tin mackerel, coconut oil, Solomon Gundy, bulla, bread biscuits and other staples. Occasionally villagers in the St. Andrew hills would ride on donkeys, mules or horses to Constant Spring, Papine, Half Way Tree and downtown Kingston to buy commodities or to sell their farm goods. This tradition went on well into the nineteen hundreds and is still a way of life in today's Jamaica.

It was on one of these road trips that a man named William Laing had a very strange but humorous experience on the road from Woodford to Constant Spring in the early twenties. He had just taken a woman named Agatha Walker in his taxi from Constant Spring to the village square named Two Trees in Woodford. After having a drink at the village bar, he drove off at about midnight and was on his way to Constant Spring. As he was nearing a little village called Congo Town he saw a man stopping him. He drove past the man resolving not to pick up anyone at that late hour. To his absolute surprise, when he looked into his rearview mirror, the stranger was seated comfortably in the back of his car. He jumped from the car but lived to tell the story with a broken foot, a broken hand, and many bruises from his bed at the public hospital in Kingston.

There were no electric lights in these villages, people would use kerosene lamps and bottle torches to see at night. Houses were made of wattle and daub. This consisted of mud plastered over bamboo and then white washed with lime. Village life was simple, the men would go to their farms during the day and work all day. Sometimes they had what was called a 'digging', where all the farmers assembled on one farm to till the soil with their pick axes, a sharp hand-plough attached to a stick.

They would work from morning till late evening and then congregate at the bar in the village square. Amidst the quattie or half a penny glass of white rum or bourbon, they would laugh, talk and drink till late at night, then go home to a proper scolding from their wives or women which made no difference as they would repeat the same thing all over again the next day.

Thursday evening was for market preparation. All the women in the village would meet in the square and load up their donkeys. One set of women would journey to Papine, while others would journey to Constant Spring. From Thursday evening to Saturday they would sell their wares then use the money to buy staples and journey back home on Saturday night. Out of these trips to the market songs like Carry Me Ackee Go Linstead Market and Woman a Heavy Load were conceived.

Farmers in these villages grew a wide variety of

produce, mainly bananas, plantain, cassava, dasheen, yam, cocoa and sugar cane. Villages like Woodford in St. Andrew had a sugar mill where every month the villagers would gather to have their sugar cane milled and the juice boiled to produce wet sugar.

The sugar would be transported to the Constant Spring market where it would be sold for a penny a pound. Farmers would also have a few animals such as goats and cows; donkeys and mules were used as beasts of burden. Everybody had common fowls in their yards. One would usually be killed for Sunday dinner. Vegetables were mainly grown by the women who took considerable pride in their vegetable gardens. Radishes, carrots, cabbages, callaloo, pak choi, and cho cho. There was also a vegetable called jokoto which grew wild and was used to supplement their dishes.

Oranges, tangerine, sweet sop, sour sop, custard apple, star apple, guava, mango, ackee, breadfruit, lemon trees and other indigenous and imported fruit trees grew in abundance on the island.

People were not wealthy, but were contented and lived happily; they respected each other's property and looked out for one another. It was unheard of for you to pass anyone without saying good morning or good evening, children couldn't whistle and let an adult hear otherwise they would get a whipping and they dared not report it to their parents, as they would receive another whipping.

When a member of the village fell ill it was everybody's affair and various remedies were suggested. In fact there was always the verbal contest as to which had the better effect: Bay rum, cerasee, vervine, cow foot, fever grass, pimento bush, lime tea; rat soup for whooping cough and a plethora of other remedies.

Whenever a member of the village died it was a major affair. Everybody had a part to play. The carpenter was responsible for making the casket, and the women would gather at the house to clean and cook. The grave would usually be dug on the Wednesday before the funeral and was usually done in the Anglican church yard or on the family plot.

In 1912 a man nicknamed Lazarus was coming home from his farm. The story told was that he stopped at the village bar and drank himself drunk. On his way home he had to pass through the Anglican cemetery. While making his way home amidst his drunken stupor, he fell into one of these freshly dug graves and fell asleep. About two o'clock in the morning he woke all sobered up and discovered that he was in a grave. Lazarus bawled out as loud as he could, and tried to grope his way out of the six-foot-six hole, but in vain. Tired and hoarse from all that shouting he finally sat down and asked himself, "But a who could a inna dem right mind bury me alive! Help! Help! Help!"

Early the next morning another man was on his way to work in Kingston. It was customary to journey before day, usually about 4–5 a.m. Having to use the cemetery as a short cut he fell into the same hole on top of Lazarus. Lazarus said to him, "Yuh come, weh yuh deh so long? Yuh know how long man a wait pon yuh."

Wings were never given to men by the Creator, but how that man flew out of that hole that Thursday morning, only God knows.

Later that morning the men in the village retrieved Lazarus from the grave with ropes, and that was how he got the name Lazarus, for they said he had risen from the dead. They also said he never drank another glass of rum.

Most funerals in the early 1900s were held on Sundays. Saturday night was the nine-night. A nine-night was celebrated nine days after the death of the individual and one day before the funeral. As to the etymology of this practice I am unclear, but it is believed that it was brought to the islands by the slaves from Africa.

A nine-night consisted of much singing and chanting, beating of drums, and drinking of hot and cold beverages like white rum, black coffee, chocolate and cocoa tea. Eating consisted of such delights as fried dumplings, fresh fish, roasted yams and a small fish known as sprat, which would be fried dry and had with white hard dough bread. Everyone attended the funeral and would give their support to the bereaved family members during and after the funeral.

When the schools came to the villages they were associated with churches such as the Anglican and Roman Catholic. There were other church schools such as the Seventh Day Adventists, Baptists and Moravian which came at a later date. While the schools were welcomed wholeheartedly by the villagers, it was dreaded by the children who attended these schools. They were trained in the practical areas of life but to comprehend the arithmetic and English was considerably difficult. In one of these schools a new teacher came from Kingston with the grand idea that these students were bright. The lesson for the day was to write a comprehension on the topic 'my ambition'. To her disappointment the poor students did not even know how to spell ambition much more to write a comprehension on the subject. On another occasion she asked one of the big boys to spell foot, he replied, "Teacher mi caa count it."

John Lemonias Seville, the principal, seldom began a statement without mentioning "We the educated". Ironically all he had as education was a senior Cambridge Certificate. Boys did not have the luxury as they do now of wearing shoes to school, they had to go barefooted.

Girls were a little more privileged and would have the use of rubber shoes. Although children had to do various chores in the morning then walk for miles to school, they could not be late for the headmaster would be there with his leather belt nicknamed 'Archie', to remind them that lateness would not be tolerated.

On two occasions the 'big boys' as they were called, got so fed up with Mr. Seville that they 'cowitched' his chair. The principal had to dismiss school early to the satisfaction of the boys, although they paid dearly the next day. On another occasion they dumped 'Archie' in the pit latrine otherwise known as the 'Jones'.

The summer holidays or 'long holidays' as it was called, was like heaven on earth for these students, especially the boys. Two months of fun and frolic from July to August. Boys would make sling shots to shoot birds, use pear seeds to make gigs, make pop guns from young bamboo shoots and use the apple blossoms for shots, and use bow and arrow and calabans to catch doves. Almost every boy would gather at blue hole on a Thursday or Sunday for a swim.

The truth was, we weren't supposed to swim in the river by law and this was strictly enforced by the district constable nicknamed Grampus. We all thought it was a stupid law, for why should boys on a hot day not take a 'headers' in the refreshing waters of blue hole. So while some boys swam, others would be on the lookout for Grampus.

But on one occasion Grampus outsmarted us. In the midst of our fun the 'watcher boys' must have forgotten to watch out for Grampus or they might have seen him coming and ran without warning the rest of us. Grampus with a wicked smile on his face, went around the rocks and took up all our clothes, then sat on the rock with a freshly cut 'sibble jack' switch in his hand.

Each boy on that judgement day got three strokes from the sibble jack, plus one running lick, the hottest of all around his wet and naked back and backside. Some ran away naked rather than face the judgement. That still didn't stop us from swimming in blue hole.

So village life in Jamaica in the late 1800s to the early 1900s was good. Hardships there were yes, but the self-reliant and entrepreneurial spirit of the ordinary Jamaican men and women who improvised amidst their rural and frugal fare is to be commended and should never be forgotten.

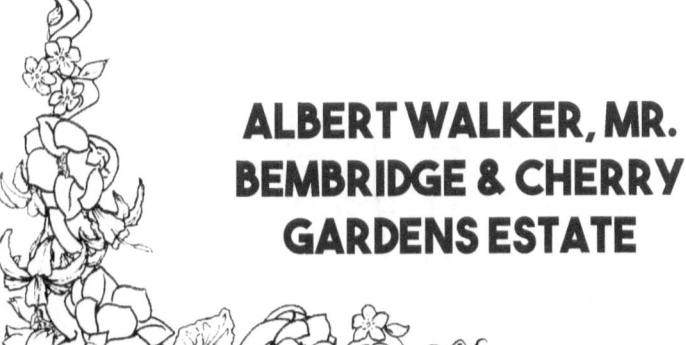

CHAPTER 1

ALBERT WALKER, MR. BEMBRIDGE & CHERRY GARDENS ESTATE

In one of the villages high above Kingston called Woodford, was a man named Albert Walker affectionately called Maas Albert. He was a leader in the village and a respectable deacon in the Anglican church. He was married to a woman called Miss Ivy and they had eight children, for men were very virile in those days and the women lively. He provided well for his family for he was the overseer at a place called Cherry Gardens Estate.

Mr. Bembridge the estate owner was a white Englishman who thought very highly of Albert Walker and took good care of him. In those days most of the Liguanea Plain was just flat grass land occupied by cattle or sugar cane amidst colonial style suburbs occupied by mostly rich Englishmen.

Mr. Bembridge's main business was in cattle, as he supplied most of Kingston with meat and milk, but he also grew tobacco and sugar cane on other estates in St. Catherine. He had a lovely house in Cherry Gardens, not very far from Constant Spring. He had four sons and a beautiful daughter named Violet.

There was a handsome black youth named Davey who was quite fond of Violet, but it was generally forbidden in those days for a black man to see or court a white man's daughter. Violet was also very fond of Davy and would steal away out to the cattle farm just to have a word with him. One day Mr. Bembridge happened to have caught them speaking to each other and gave Davy a firm talking to, while scolding Violet and threatening to send her to England to her aunt Hilda.

Violet's love for Davy was strong and amidst the remonstrations of her father, she continued to see Davy. Her room on the great house was a lovely room at the side of the house with big French windows. She told Davy that to get her attention in the late evenings, he should put a stick through the window and poke the mattress three times, then she would sneak out to him. This they kept up for weeks until Mr. Bembridge learnt of it. One night he laid down on his daughter's bed and waited for Davy. When Davy pushed the stick through the window, it landed straight on Mr. Bembridge's chest. Mr. Bembridge and two of his servants leaped through the window and tried to grab him. The young man ran that night from Cherry Gardens straight to Spanish Town and was never seen again. Violet was later sent off to England to her aunt and to school.

Mr. Bembridge had many servants employed to him and took very good care of his affairs. He was a kind hearted gentleman and a Christian who looked out for his servants. Maas Albert was in charge of his estate at Cherry Gardens. His main job was to supervise the cattle boys, tally the milk and ensure that it was properly collected and transported to the condenser. He also oversaw the butchering of cattle and ensured that it was properly salted and cured for distribution. Occasionally Mr. Bembridge would take him on horseback to St. Catherine where he also did jobs on the sugar estate near Spanish Town.

Maas Albert was paid well or so it was rumored for he was one of the few men in Woodford who had a board house complete with verandah and glass windows. He could also read and write, and so would assist the parson at the Anglican church with the preaching. The journey from Woodford to Cherry Gardens Estate was fifteen miles. Given the state of the roads in those days, travelling was considerably difficult. Most roads were just little tracks and roads to the hills were treacherous and lined with dangerous precipices, especially in the hills of St. Andrew. Maas Albert would wake up before day and be at his job by 8 a.m. Most times he would spend the week at the estate before heading home to his wife on Friday. There was a shortcut from Woodford through a place called Norbrook near Constant Spring, which shortened the journey through Papine and allowed people to get from the hills to Constant Spring or Liguanea very quickly.

In those days Papine was a small town consisting of a Chinese shop from which you could get most of your groceries. There was also a post office, police station and market. There were a number of smaller shops such as cook and clothes shops which lined the streets. There was a main road from Papine which went all the way to Half Way Tree and branched out into Spanish Town and Kingston Harbour. Cars were few and those who had them were greatly admired. Most people travelled on horseback, rail or tram cars from Constant Spring to Kingston.

CHAPTER 2

MAAS ALBERT BECAME ILL

Jamaica at the time was free from diseases such as cholera, but the disease was still dreaded since it wreaked havoc on the island in 1851-1853. Some forty thousand persons were killed and those who lived to tell the tale saw every major disease as a reminder of the dreaded cholera. Jamaica's cholera outbreak was part of the second cholera pandemic, known as the Asiatic cholera pandemic, which ran from 1829 to 1851 and reached Europe including London and Paris in 1832. Jamaica's death toll was high, 40,000 deaths, one-tenth of the island's 400,000 population. It was noted that few countries hit by cholera at the time surpassed Jamaica's cholera death rate.

Dr. Parkin's at the time remarkably detailed the account of the outbreak as he travelled throughout the island treating patients. He wrote that from Port Royal, where the first cases were found, the disease spread quickly to Kingston, affecting 6,000 people of a population of 40,000.

Parkins noted, "It (cholera) prevailed in this town (Kingston), in a severe form, for about six weeks; and, during this period, spread with unusual rapidity to other parts of the island. The first fatal case in Kingston was on the 11th October; on the 19th there were three deaths in the adjoining parish St Catherine and, on the following day, Dr. Palmer, of Spanish Town, who, in conjunction with four other practitioners, had made a post-mortem of one of the bodies, was attacked, and died in a few hours."

The death toll from cholera rapidly continued in Spanish Town, at the time the capital of Jamaica, with 30 deaths on October 20, and Parkins noted that cholera continued "Its destructive career" in the capital until the end of November. He noted "Few towns having been more severely visited than this, the capital of Jamaica".

"It appeared at St. Thomas, in the east, thirty miles from Kingston, on the other side, about the same time as at Spanish Town; and from these different points it spread east, west, north, and south. By the end of November, it had reached every part of the island, excepting the parish of Manchester, in the center, and the parishes of Westmoreland and Hanover, situated at the western and north-western extremity of the island", Parkins wrote.

The "Essential symptoms of cholera" as observed by Parkins in his 1851 notes were "The collapsed countenance; blueness of the body, particularly in Europeans, but scarcely perceptible in the negro; shrunken fingers; wrinkled, shriveled skin; total suspension of all secretions particularly the biliary, foecal, and renal, the non-generation of animal heat, with icy coldness of the extremities and tongue; arrest of the circulation, and total cessation of the pulse".

Parkins complained about shortage of drugs and supplies and just the great difficulty in getting the correct medical supplies. It appeared, though, that he was a resourceful doctor and quickly learned to make do with what was available.

Transmission to humans occurred through eating food or drinking water contaminated with Vibrio cholerae from other cholera patients. It was characterized by severe diarrhea with extreme fluid losses which could result in dehydration and electrolyte loss that could lead to death.

Besides watery diarrhea, other symptoms included vomiting, abdominal pain, rapid heart rate, dry skin and sometimes fever. The symptoms of cholera were well known in Jamaica so when people came down with vomiting and diarrhea it was often diagnosed as cholera, and doctors would take extra precaution and administer seltzer or soda water as a cure.

One evening Maas Albert came home to his wife and complained of not feeling well. She dutifully boiled him some vervine with ginger and put him to bed. Later that night he came down with a terrible fever and had to strip himself of his clothes. He woke up in the morning feeling a little better and insisted on going to work despite the protest from his wife. Maas Albert prided himself in being a 'man' and was not one to give in easily to a woman. He said goodbye to his wife and as usual he would not be back till Friday evening. "Tek care Albert," she said as he mounted his mule. As he rode his mule nicknamed Lyder through the village before day that Tuesday morning, he felt the cool breeze on his face and was determined not to let this little malady or so he thought, prevent him from going to his work.

He arrived at Cherry Gardens Estate about 7:30 a.m. and found Mr. Bembridge attending to the cows. Mr. Bembridge called out, "Albert, you are here."

"Yes sah," replied Maas Albert.

"Early as usual," said Mr. Bembridge.

"Only my duty sah," replied Maas Albert, as he dismounted from Lyder and led her to the horse peg. He went into the shed, changed into his work clothes and boots, then went out to Mr. Bembridge.

By eight o'clock all the workers had arrived. Maas Albert gave the usual instructions, which involved dispatching some to milk the cows, and ensuring that it was properly measured in gallon tins as well as counted. They would then be packed onto a cart and sent to the condensery in Kingston. There were about forty cows to be milked, plus another eighty on the grass which Mr. Bembridge occasionally slaughtered, mostly the bulls for meat. There were also dozens of goats on the property which were attended to by young boys.

That morning Mr. Bembridge's property was abuzz with activity. The cook Miss Babsy, was a stout Maroon woman from Portland who took care of the meals. People said that she was the best cook in Kingston. She was responsible for all meals prepared on the property. At 8:30 a.m. she would prepare the breakfast which consisted sometimes of run 'dung' with dumplings, peppered salt fish, steamed fresh fish, yam, bread, porridge, coffee tea and salt fish fritters.

Lunch time was usually the best part of the day and would commence from 12:30 to about 2:00 p.m. Mr. Bembridge always had guests over for lunch. Sometimes merchants and businessmen in Kingston would stop over for a day and would praise Miss Babsy for her culinary skills.

Dinner at Mr. Bembridge's home usually consisted of roast pork, curried mutton, stewed or roasted beef, rice and gungu peas, corn pone, sweet potato pudding, vegetables, and always there would be Madeira wine, white rum and coconut water. The servants would be served sugar water and lime which they called 'wash'. Sometimes Miss Babsy would put a little bourbon or white rum in the wash to keep up their spirits, something they liked very much.

Maas Albert was doing his usual rounds when he felt very weak in the knees. Not wanting to show any weakness, he continued working but found it considerably difficult. He held on to the fence that surrounded the cows with both hands and found himself sweating profusely. He knew that something was terribly wrong but tried to keep up a brave front. One of the farmhands named Zekel noticed that Maas Albert was not looking himself. He came over to where Maas Albert was supporting himself by leaning on the fence.

"Yuh aright sah?"

Maas Albert didn't respond.

"Maas Albert! Yuh aright?"

Still no response.

Zekel was just in time to catch Maas Albert as he collapsed to the ground. Zekel wasted no time in calling some of the men on the farm to help lift Maas Albert to the work shed. By this time a young man ran to the great house to inform Mr. Bembridge that Maas Albert "Faint weh".

Mr. Bembridge was having dinner that afternoon with guests from Spanish Town and was not very urgent on the matter, for he thought that Maas Albert had gotten sun stroke and would soon get over it. He told Miss Babsy to send a gallon of wash and white rum to the shed with the hope that Maas Albert would soon revive. The men put Maas Albert down on the crude mattress made of coir and went back to their work. They didn't wish to get too comfortable with him, as he was somewhat socially distant from them.

Mr. Bembridge didn't reach the shed until well after three o'clock that evening. What he saw shocked him. Apart from the fact that Maas Albert was groaning in pain, his face contorted and his body boiling with fever, there was a dark hue which came over him, and the bed bugs from the coir mattress were crawling all over him.

"My God, Albert! Albert! I didn't know you were so ill, what is wrong with you?"

Poor Maas Albert only groaned in pain. Storming out of the shed he called Miss Babsy, "Babsy! Quick! Fix up the backroom, heat some water and pour it in the trough."

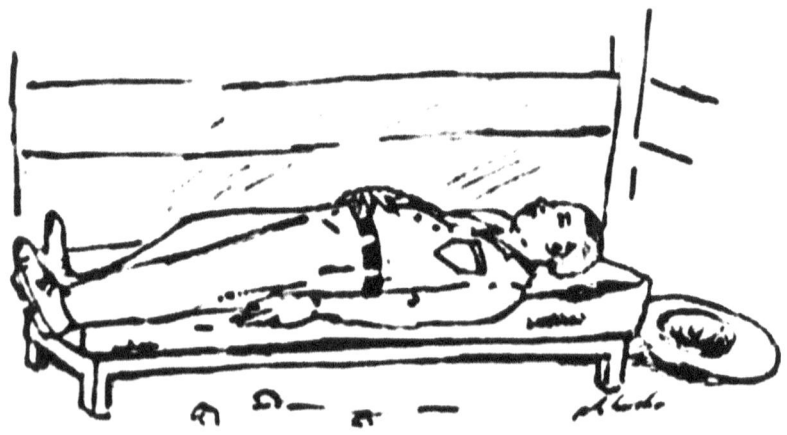

The commands were obeyed with much urgency, for Mr. Bembridge although a nice man, would sometimes rule with magisterial authority. By late evening Maas Albert was washed, clothed in clean white bed clothes and lying on a soft bed in the back room. Miss Babsy brought him some chicken soup but he soon vomited it up; there was nothing they gave him that he did not bring up.

CHAPTER 3

JOURNEY TO SPANISH TOWN TO SEE DR. BENJAMIN

M r. Bembridge was in consternation, thinking this and thinking that. Then the dreaded thought came to him, *I wonder if this is cholera*? He trembled at the thought. He was aware of the devastating effects this disease had had on Jamaica years ago. If this was cholera, then this could be the end of him and his house for this disease was very contagious. He immediately gave orders for the work shed to be cleaned. The coir bed was removed and a fresh bed was put there. Maas Albert slept little that night, and the next morning found him worse. He was still roasting with fever, his joints pained and along with the vomiting, he had diarrhea.

Mr. Bembridge called one of his men, a trusted messenger whose name was Jones. "Jones I want you to ride to Spanish Town as quickly as you can. Go straight to Dr. Benjamin and hand him this letter."

Jones wasted no time in obeying his master's command. But the journey from Cherry Gardens to Spanish Town was a long one. He left Cherry Gardens Estate that morning at 10:30, but didn't arrive in Spanish Town until well after three o'clock that evening. He found Dr. Benjamin busy attending to patients at his office. He was a well-known doctor and was reputed to be quite rich.

He was one of the few men in Jamaica at the time who owned a motor car and it would cause considerable stir when he drove through Spanish Town.

Jones handed the letter to Dr. Benjamin. He sat in a chair, put on his spectacles and gingerly opened the letter.

"Would you excuse me for a while?"

Jones who was standing respectfully at the door went out from the office. There was a pound note neatly folded in the envelope which the doctor did not wish for Jones to see.

The letter read "Come as quickly as you can, my farm manager is very ill. Symptoms look like cholera."

Dr. Benjamin chuckled softly. *Looks like every sickness is cholera these days; anyway I will not be able to attend to him till Thursday for I have a very important meeting with the governor tomorrow.* He handed Jones another letter, gave him a few shillings to buy food and drinks, and told him to ride back to Cherry Gardens Estate before day the next morning. The letter stated briefly that he would arrive on Thursday afternoon of that week to attend to Maas Albert.

By Wednesday night Maas Albert had gotten progressively worse, he hadn't eaten much and was vomiting profusely. Poor Miss Babsy tried everything she knew to stop his vomiting. She tried ginger tea, she tried vervine and parched flour to stop his diarrhea, and there were other remedies that Mr. Bembridge administered but to no avail. He grew pale and had the look of death on his face.

When Mr. Bembridge visited the shed Thursday morning Maas Albert was almost at death's door. He was breathing but it was a heavy laboured breathing with rapid gasps of breaths. He was trying to say something to

Mr. Bembridge but could hardly speak. Mr. Bembridge asked in as kind a voice as he could, "What is it you want to say to me?"

Maas Albert's lips moved but no sound came. Miss Babsy came over and read his lips. She straightened herself, took one look at Mr. Bembridge and said with a sad note in her voice, "He asking for his wife Ivy sar."

"My God!" said Mr. Bembridge. "I never thought of it, I must send a message to his dear wife and children but not before Dr. Benjamin examines him."

CHAPTER 4

DR. BENJAMIN'S VISIT TO CHERRY GARDENS ESTATE

Dr. Benjamin left Spanish Town about eight o'clock that morning and reached Cherry Gardens Estate about eleven o'clock. He drove a blue Edwardian-style sedan. It was one of the few cars on the island at the time and the people looked at it as though it were a supernatural sight. When he roared into Cherry Gardens Estate the men and boys stopped their work and gazed in wonder at the car.

Mr. Bembridge was waiting impatiently, stomping up and down the porch with his hands behind him. He greeted Dr. Benjamin warmly, but subtly scolded him for not coming at once.

"Good to see you Bembridge, it's been quite a while, I trust you're well. I would have come from yesterday but

I had a very important meeting with the governor yesterday. I sent a letter with your horseman Jones."

"Yes, yes," said Mr. Bembridge. "I received your letter yesterday afternoon."

The two men entered the great hall at the front porch and sat down. Miss Babsy brought a drink of Madeira wine and beef sandwiches. Mr. Bembridge would have none except a drink of the wine. Dr. Benjamin who was exhausted from the drive, took time to have his snack while questioning Mr. Bembridge about the sick. After the short meal, Mr. Bembridge led Dr. Benjamin to the shed where Maas Albert was.

The large wooden windows in the shed were opened so there was enough sunlight shining through. Dr. Benjamin walked gingerly over to the bed while Mr. Bembridge stood in the doorway. He took his trumpet from his doctor's bag and placed it on Maas Albert's chest; he then used his fingers to open Maas Albert's eyes. With a shaky voice he stood and exclaimed, "I am afraid you're right Bembridge, these are the symptoms of cholera."

Mr. Bembridge was dumbstruck. He didn't say much but listened aghast as Dr. Benjamin spoke.

"The man is almost dead Bembridge, and we all may be dead by morning if you don't take the necessary precautions. He must be taken to the cholera cemetery and buried at once, and this shed and mattress must be burnt immediately to prevent the disease from spreading."

"My God!" said Mr. Bembridge, "but the man is not yet dead."

"Trust me," said Dr. Benjamin, "he will live for two or three hours the most. After that he is gone, and it will do us all good; in fact it will do this country good if we dispose of his body properly before we have another outbreak of cholera. Do you remember what happened in 1851? Surely we wouldn't want that repeated, would we?"

The doctor took a look at his wrist watch, then said to Mr. Bembridge, "Sorry, I was hoping to spend the night but under the circumstances I have to go. You must take every precaution to properly dispose of this man's body immediately."

With that said Dr. Benjamin got into his car and roared out of Cherry Gardens Estate.

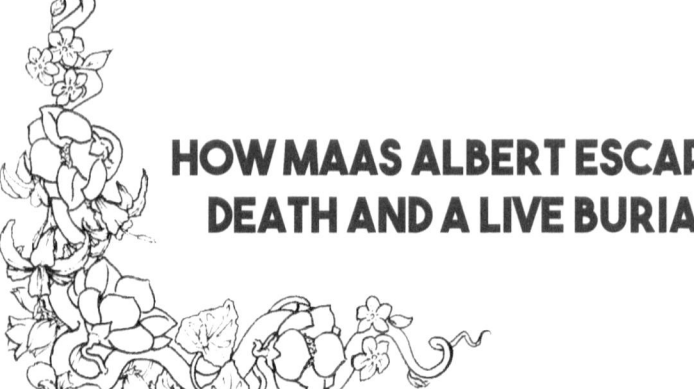

CHAPTER 5

HOW MAAS ALBERT ESCAPED DEATH AND A LIVE BURIAL

Mr. Bembridge read exactly into what the doctor was saying. With mixed feelings he sent a message to the Superintendent of Police, a white Englishman at Half Way Tree police station known as Starkey. Superintendent Starkey was about to go at once to Cherry Gardens Estate, for he always liked visiting there, but when he learnt that it was a case of cholera he opted to send the ill-tempered Corporal Glenford Sharpe, nicknamed Robusta. He was a short, stocky black man with a high forehead, thick mustache and strong hands. It was rumored that he once arrested a man and snapped the man's hands with the force of his hold. The permission was given for burial without hesitation and to take all necessary precautions to contain the disease.

Corporal Sharpe arrived at Cherry Gardens Estate about three o'clock and was very upset that Superintendent Starkey had entrusted him with such a task. Mr. Bembridge with much sadness provided four men to assist Corporal Sharpe with the task of disposing of the body. Albert Walker was covered with a white sheet, and laid on a crude stretcher made from bamboo poles with a strong flour-bag sheet tied between the poles.

Four men carried the makeshift stretcher. They had shovels to dig the grave at the cholera cemetery near Constant Spring. The shed at Cherry Gardens Estate in which Maas Albert had stayed during his sickness, along with the mattress, were later burnt.

Mr. Bembridge, his wife, Miss Babsy, and all of the employees and servants at Cherry Gardens Estate had tears in their eyes as Corporal Sharpe and the four men marched away from there to the cholera cemetery in Constant Spring with Maas Albert's body.

The road from Cherry Gardens to Constant Spring went through a place called Norbrook. To get to Norbrook in those days, one had to walk through Jacks Hill, then down into Constant Spring. Norbrook had a river which ran from the hills of St. Andrew which was really a tributary of the Wag Water river. It was while coming down from Jacks Hill to Constant Spring that Maas Albert started groaning. The men carrying the body hastily dropped the bamboo carrier and ran a distance for they thought he was already dead.

Corporal Sharpe with a roar, was demanding that they return to their duty, when Maas Albert in a weak and mournful voice started speaking. "Duh tek time wid mi, mi nuh dead yet."

Corporal Sharpe would have none of it. "Mi say yuh dead!" Although weak and almost at the point of death, Maas Albert understood what was happening to him. A deadly chill came over him. He saw his lovely wife Ivy, his children, especially little six-year old Suzie, who would run to meet him each time he came home. With the little strength he had left, he renewed his protest. "Duh sah, tek time wid mi, mi nuh dead."

But Corporal Sharpe, like an angry and stubborn bull, replied, "Shut yuh mouth man, dead man tell no tales." The truth was that Corporal Sharpe had already been paid to bury Maas Albert and would have the job done whether Maas Albert was dead or alive.

Poor Maas Albert realized that his protest was futile. He would be buried whether he liked it or not and perhaps alive. The procession was now going through the Jacks Hill area; it was about minutes to six now and was almost dark. Maas Albert with the dread of his live burial looming, tried to get up from the flour-bag stretcher, but was too weak. He tried to speak but no sound came from his lips. He prayed earnestly. *Please God help me, don't let dem bury me alive, at least let me die first.* With the prayer on his lips, and with all the strength he could muster, Maas Albert heaved himself and rolled off the stretcher.

Over the precipice he went and rolled like a rock down the hillside. Corporal Sharpe, who was walking in front of the men who carried the stretcher, turned around at the commotion and rained a string of bad words on them.

"Why oonuh mek him get way?"

The men did not reply but gazed in horror at the white ghost-looking body of Maas Albert rolling further down the precipice. After a few minutes of silence one of the men replied, "Boss him can't live, him just bury himself." Corporal Sharpe reckoned that he was right. There was no way Maas Albert could live going down that hillside. He paid the men ten shillings each and sent them home. He charged them strictly to tell Mr. Bembridge that Maas Albert's body was buried in Jacks Hill for night came down and they did not reach Constant Spring in time.

Corporal Sharpe reached Cherry Gardens Estate about ten o'clock that night. He gave a full report to Mr. Bembridge, then returned to his post at the Half Way Tree police station. The following day he also gave a full report to Superintendent Starkey.

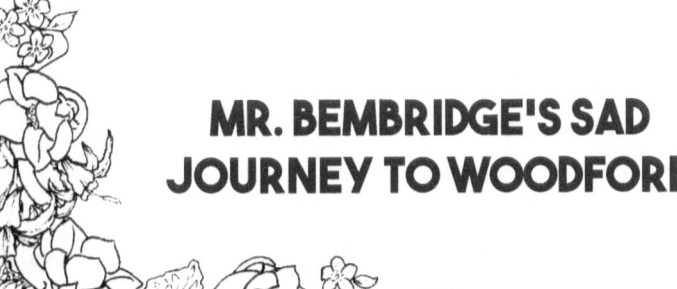

CHAPTER 6

MR. BEMBRIDGE'S SAD JOURNEY TO WOODFORD

The next morning being Friday, Mr. Bembridge came from his great house very tired for he slept very little that night. The first thing on his mind was how to get a message to Woodford. How would he be able to tell poor Miss Ivy the sad news? No doubt she was expecting her dear husband to be home Friday evening and would boil his nice cock soup as usual. How sad that on the day she expected to welcome her husband home, she would instead receive news of his death. Mr. Bembridge and two of his men made ready for the journey from Cherry Gardens to Woodford. They left Cherry Gardens Estate that morning about eight o'clock. They rode on three horses, with Maas Albert's faithful Lyder towing behind. They went through the Liguanea Plain on towards Papine. They would have taken the regular route which was from Cherry Gardens through Norbrook to a place called Peter's Rock and then Woodford, but rain had fallen the night before and it was very treacherous to cross the river at Constant Spring. Also the roads were in a deplorable condition, so they opted to ride through Papine bypassing Gordon Town into Irish Town. When they reached Irish Town they headed for the barracks at Newcastle; there they stopped to buy food and drink.

Newcastle at the time was one of the major barracks on the island; there were about four hundred soldiers both in training as well as the reserves. They were stationed there under the leadership of General Gomm.

They left Newcastle about twelve noon. They rode through Hollywell and headed for the two-mile trip downhill to Woodford. When they entered the village people stared at them for it was very unusual to see a white man in the village. A little boy showed them the way to Maas Albert's house which was a little distance from the village square, on a hill overlooking the village of Woodford. It was a small, neat house fitted with glass window squares and a verandah at the front. It was painted brown and the walls were sand dashed. Miss Ivy was busy inside making preparations for her husband as she expected him about four to five o'clock each Friday evening.

When Mr. Bembridge and his two men arrived at the house their horses neighed and came to a halt. Maas Albert's little daughter Suzie ran towards the gate shouting

"Papa, papa come!" Poor little Suzie couldn't understand why it was not her father. She stood dumbfounded looking up into the face of Mr. Bembridge and his two men who by now had dismounted their horses. Miss Ivy and two of her boys soon followed and were equally troubled to see a white man and two somber looking black men at the gate. Lyder, Maas Albert's mule was there but where was her husband? Mrs. Ivy Walker was a nice looking brown woman, stoutly built with a beautiful smile. She kept her house tidy and had her children under subjection. When she wasn't attending her vegetable garden, she was busy sewing or cooking. She was well loved in the village. She stood with her hands akimbo, as Mr. Bembridge and his men approached the gate.

"Mrs. Walker, I presume," said Mr. Bembridge.

"Yes sir and who are you?"

"I am William Bembridge, Albert's employer."

A shiver ran down Miss Ivy's spine as she asked in a trembling voice, "And why are you here sir?"

Not willing to startle poor Miss Ivy, Mr. Bembridge began to praise Maas Albert. "I have always wanted to meet the wife of Albert Walker, he is the best estate manager I've ever had. Under his watch Cherry Gardens Estate has prospered so much, my pleasure to meet you Miss Ivy."

"Please sar, tell me what happen to Albert, him supposed to be coming home this evening as he always does."

Mr. Bembridge straightened himself and looked Miss Ivy straight in the eye. A trickle of sweat ran down his face. Hat in both hands he said, "I am afraid Mrs. Walker, he won't be coming home. Albert died yesterday of cholera and had to be buried quickly, so as not to spread the disease."

There was a loud thud as Miss Ivy fainted on the verandah. Poor little Suzie started screaming, thinking that these strange men had done something to her mother.

By the time Miss Ivy was revived, the entire village had congregated at Maas Albert's place. There was Maas Joe, Isaac Jackson, Levi Walker, Daniel Clemetson and Father Paul. Some of the women had already gone to market and would not hear about Maas Albert until Saturday night.

Mr. Bembridge wasted no time in telling the full story to the villagers. Miss Ivy was inconsolable, she just wept and wept. Her children wept for 'Papa' as he was affectionately called, the villagers wept, even the parson wept; for Maas Albert was a leader and well beloved in the village of Woodford. Mr. Bembridge and his men slept in the village that night at the parson's home, during which time they made hasty preparations for Albert's memorial service which would be the next Sunday.

Early Saturday morning before leaving Woodford for Cherry Gardens Estate, Mr. Bembridge visited Miss Ivy. She was at home surrounded by some of the women in the village. He took her to a room in the house to have a private conversation with her.

"Mrs. Walker all these years Albert has been a faithful worker, very honest, very diligent, and a disciplined gentleman; it's not going to be easy to replace him. Anyway kindly take this, as a token of gratitude for your husband's work", at which Mr. Bembridge placed two hundred pounds in Miss Ivy's hand.

"Thank you sar." Miss Ivy had never seen so much money in all her life. Indeed Maas Albert had never brought home ten pounds since he started working at Cherry Gardens Estate. In those days ten pounds could buy land, but two hundred pounds! A beautiful smile came over her face as she reached for a thread bag, folded the notes and promptly put them in her bosom. That done, Mr. Bembridge and his men rode off for home at Cherry Gardens Estate.

By Saturday night the entire village was present at Maas Albert's home. People from as far as Papine heard the sad news and came to give their condolences. The women in the village wasted no time to take charge of affairs at Maas Albert's house. Some cleaned the house, others washed, some cooked for the men who were playing dominoes, and Miss Ivy was both sad and glad at the same time. With all the consolation she was receiving her heart went out in thanksgiving to God and to Mr. Bembridge, who had just made her rich. She couldn't take her mind off the two hundred pounds which was tied securely in her bosom. Yes, she missed her dear husband but what a blessing his death had brought her. Should she leave Woodford and buy a house in Kingston? Should she send her sons to England to study to be barristers, or should she build a bigger house?

Who would have thought that her husband's death would bring her so much money?

She held her bosom and came out to the women who were attending her house.

CHAPTER 7

RESCUED BY TWO RASTAFARIANS

Maas Albert's body came to rest in a small stream at the bottom of the precipice. From Jacks Hill all the way down to Norbrook, near a village called Congo Town. It was absolutely unbelievable for a man to slide over these treacherous gullies without seriously harming or killing himself. Perhaps it was the tremendous amount of guinea grass that lined the hillsides, but for Maas Albert being a preacher, he attributed it to the protection of God.

From Thursday night, to all day Friday and now Saturday morning, Maas Albert lay in the shallow stream waiting for death. He was so weak he couldn't even get himself out of the shallow stream which he was lying in. There was pain all over his battered body, but especially his shoulder which he hit on a rock when he fell down the precipice. He managed to drink water from the stream, by sucking up water with his lips.

Poor Albert groaned. "God!" he said, "what this is on me?" Weak as he was his mind was alert but he was going in and out of consciousness. He prayed again. *Oh God have mercy on me.*

That morning two Rasta men, Ras Jeremiah and Ras Benjie were on their way to look wicker to make baskets and brooms, when they came upon the body of Maas Albert. Thinking that he was dead, they were making their way around the body when Maas Albert groaned.

"But this man nuh dead, but a how him reach dung yah so. It look like him fall offa de road and drop dung inna Zion yah, we haffi help him," said Ras Jeremiah, "for although him a baldhead a still Selassie son."

"True I," said Ras Benjie.

Maas Albert was soon placed on a makeshift stretcher made with withes and latched unto two bamboo sticks, and carried into the Rasta men's camp at Congo Town.

"It nuh look like him a go live Benjie bwoy, him look bad, but mek we try wid him," said Ras Jeremiah. Maas Albert was placed in a hammock, in a hut with a thatched roof. He was given water and a stupefying mixture of green vervine juice.

The next morning Ras Jeremiah and Ras Benjie started working in earnest to revive Maas Albert. They got seven different kinds of herbs: vervine root, rosemary, briar withes, cerasee, cowfoot, ginger, sarsaparilla and fever grass. They chopped them up, then beat them with a mortar and pestle. The juice from this concoction was strained, mixed with honey and given to Maas Albert to drink. In the mornings they would boil pumpkin soup with dove meat and feed him with a spoon. For three weeks he lay in the hammock, until he felt a little better and could sit up for a few minutes. When he was sufficiently revived he asked Ras Jeremiah, "A weh mi deh?"

Ras Jeremiah with much satisfaction at his progress started to relate the story, but poor Maas Albert went back to sleep before the story was over.

After two weeks he was strong enough and eventually learned of his unfortunate ordeal. He then related to Ras Jeremiah how he came down with cholera, that he was the farm manager at Cherry Gardens Estate and how they were on their way to bury him when he rolled off the stretcher and ended up in the Norbrook river.

CHAPTER 8

NINE-NIGHT AND FUNERAL

Two weeks after Maas Albert's ordeal, the villagers in Woodford had his nine-night. It started about nine o'clock Saturday night and ended early Sunday morning. It was probably one of the most well attended wakes in St. Andrew. Many of the workers from Cherry Gardens Estate had travelled from Friday evening and lodged at various places in Woodford, some even slept at the school; for the villagers had lodged most of the travellers from Kingston and Spanish Town. Maas Albert had relatives in St. Thomas who started travelling from early Thursday morning. Miss Babsy the cook at Cherry Gardens Estate, was busy in Miss Ivy's kitchen.

Sprat and fresh fish were bought in abundance at Papine market and carried on donkeys to Woodford, along with fried dumplings, roasted yellow yams, cock soup, dozens of white hard dough bread, bammy, and bottles upon bottles of white rum, strong ale and bourbon. Coffee, chocolate tea, peppered salt fish and run 'dung' were prepared. It was estimated that between three hundred to four hundred persons were present at the wake. Even some of the soldiers from Newcastle were present, for Albert often journeyed through Newcastle to Woodford and made friends with many of the soldiers there.

The singing and chanting which began Saturday went on into the early hours of Sunday morning. The drums' beat while the men and women sang the old African spirituals like A Albert Mek We Deh Ya, We All Have To Part One Day, Nobody Can Go Into Maas Albert Room, and No Grave Cannot Hold My Body Down. They exhausted every song in the book amidst eating and drinking, and dancing and talking. Sunday morning found several drunken men staggering home, while some were fast asleep in the grass which lined the roadside.

The memorial service started at approximately two-thirty that Sunday afternoon. The Anglican church at Woodford was packed to capacity and overflowed into the church yard and street. Among those present were Mr. and Mrs. Bembridge, Miss Babsy, and several people of note in the congregation. Miss Ivy, her sons and two daughters, little Suzie and Elizabeth were of course front and center. Miss Ivy wore her beautiful lace black dress and looked very somber, with Mrs. Bembridge seated beside her. She was weeping profusely at the turn of events but mostly because she didn't even get to see her husband for the last time. Mr. Bembridge gave a moving tribute in which he spoke of Maas Albert's qualities, how he was always on time, how honest he was and how he managed the estate with efficiency. There were several other tributes given by friends and relatives.

The English Anglican bishop Father Paul led the sermon.

Dearly beloved, friends and family of the deceased, Mr. and Mrs. Bembridge of Cherry Gardens Estate with whose presence we are highly honored, citizens of this beautiful little village of Woodford benighted by the sudden loss of our friend, brother and member of this church, Sister Ivy beloved wife of our brother, good afternoon!

In 1851 over 40,000 of our citizens perished because of cholera, I was very sad to hear that our dearly departed brother Albert perished because of this malady. I would hope that this isn't another outbreak, but if it is, we must take it very seriously. Death and destruction may show itself again. Therefore let us turn to God with all our hearts for no man knows who will be next. Today it is Albert, but tomorrow it could be you or even me...

With many words he exhorted, comforted and even condemned. He ended the memorial service with the singing of the hymn In The Sweet By And By. There wasn't any burial, so the people disbursed themselves to their homes, the men to the rum bars and others travelled the next morning to Kingston and other places. Miss Ivy though very sad, was satisfied that everything went well.

CHAPTER 9

ALBERT WALKER IN THE RASTAFARIAN CAMP

It was now four weeks since Ras Jeremiah and Ras Benjie had found Maas Albert in the little stream at the bottom of Norbrook. He was still weak and had a bit of difficulty walking but he was able to speak. One morning he expressed his desire to leave, a longing to see his family, but Ras Jeremiah protested.

"You haffi tek Rasta medicine fi seven weeks and you only gone four, you have three more weeks fi go, so jus' relax! Jah say seven different herbs, seven days a week for seven weeks; after dat de I wi betta."

Maas Albert protested further but eventually saw the Rasta man's point. One morning he attempted to walk but was so weak he stumbled and had to be helped back to his hammock. Ras Jeremiah continued his round of medication. Two times a day, seven different herbs and Maas Albert progressively grew better. The dullness had gone from his eyes, the bluish-black color had gone from his skin and he was really looking the picture of health except for the weakness in his knees and hands.

It was surmised that Maas Albert had come down with malaria or yellow fever. Had he contracted cholera he would have certainly died and those who handled him would have probably caught the disease. Ras Jeremiah although not a physician, confirmed that his sickness was not cholera. Even though Maas Albert was sick the two Rasta men were honored to have him as their guest and would tell story after story each evening. They talked about slavery, Africa and they even discussed the Bible, and would reason late into the night. The two Rasta men Albert learnt, had their women and children in Congo Town and would visit them every now and then.

They grew a wide variety of crops, mainly vegetables which they would sell at the Constant Spring market. They also made baskets, mats and brooms from wicker. They'd leave early on Thursday mornings and would not get back till Friday afternoon. They bought various things for their farms and replenished their food supplies.

CHAPTER 10

LONELY DAYS AND NIGHTS FOR MISS IVY

Back in Woodford, Miss Ivy was getting used to the absence of her husband. In the evenings she would sometimes cry herself to sleep. Her children would gather round and comfort her as best they could, as well as some of her friends in the village. It did little at first but with time she accepted the fact and was determined to move on with her life. She journeyed one morning to Kingston to the central bank where she deposited most of the two hundred pounds Mr. Bembridge had given her. She made herself busy and would pay the men in the village to do her farming. But occasionally she would have very depressing and sad episodes when she remembered her Albert.

Her children did the best they could without their father; the bigger boys attended to his farm, while the younger boys saw to his goats. Suzie the little six-year old, constantly asked for 'papa'. Every mule or horse which passed the house Suzie would dart outside shouting "Papa come!" Poor Miss Ivy tried to tell her that papa would not be coming home. There were nights when she just wept and wept and the children tried to comfort her but to no avail.

One night she prayed aloud, "Massa God, it hard pan mi. How mi fi live without Albert? How de pickney dem gwine manage without dem father? Imagine not even a proper burial fi mi look upon mi husband face fi de last time! You just tek him from mi so! Lawd God weh mi a go do? Lawd if it possible bring him back for might as well mi dead without Albert."

God must have heard that prayer for one night after crying herself to sleep, she had a strange dream about her husband. He was looking healthy and strong and was telling her to make cock soup for he was coming home early Friday evening.

Miss Ivy awakened out of her sleep and went into depression when she realized it was only a dream. A loving old lady named Mother Grant would come over from time to time. She was known as the prayer warrior in the village and would take the time to comfort poor Miss Ivy.

"God knows best mi child, leave it in the hands of God", she would say to Miss Ivy.

It was common rum talk among the men in the bar at the square as to who would take over Maas Albert's wife. Some even proposed leaving their women for her. She was a beautiful woman and furthermore it was rumored that she was rich. Poor Miss Ivy had no peace. Almost every evening one of these men would make a pass at her, especially one named Maas White who would say, "Ivy, Albert dead, and you need a man to tek charge of affairs and I think I am the right one fi you." Another one would offer to show her his yam ground, he boasted the best renta and St. Vincent yams. Perhaps that was his way of convincing her as to his ability to take care of her.

One morning a fight broke out at her gate. A man named Charlie Bates took some freshly cut callaloo and carrots to Miss Ivy. Maas White rode up on his mule just in time to hear Charlie calling Miss Ivy.

"Weh you want wid de woman, you nuh see she grieving?"

Charlie responded, "Mi owe you? Why you don't mind you blooming business? You no have Lurlene and you hungry belly pickney dem fi mind?"

Maas White dismounted his mule and drew his machete. Charlie had to run like a mad man, for Maas White was temporarily insane. "If a ever catch you a skin you alive, don't come back a de woman gate."

Poor Miss Ivy was quite affected by the turn of events. She began making preparations to leave Woodford and to start life somewhere else.

CHAPTER 11

MAAS ALBERT'S RETURN TO WOODFORD

After seven weeks living with the Rasta men in Norbrook, Maas Albert was looking the picture of health, the weakness had gone and he felt like a new man. He would walk around the little hut and help the men with their farming. The two Rastas congratulated themselves on being good bush doctors. One morning Maas Albert looked up to Peter's Rock mountain and sighed. "I must go home to my wife and children," he said to Ras Jeremiah who was the elder of the two Rasta men.

"True I, the time has come. After seven weeks of I and I herbs, the most High give thee health and strength to return to thy people. Return mi brethren for I sure they longing after you."

Maas Albert had by now gotten used to this type of talking but this time he sensed a kind of prophetic sincerity in the Rasta man's voice. A tear ran down his cheek as he reflected on how kind they were to him. Were it not for these two men, he would have died.

They dressed Maas Albert in white pants and a long white Rasta gown that came down to his ankles. These were the only clothes he had, since he left Cherry Gardens Estate in his night clothes, and after seven weeks they were useless. They packed a little provision of cashew nuts and dried herbs in a small thread bag which he slung over his left shoulder, and they also gave him a long stick with which to walk. They went with him from Norbrook through Congo Town up to Peter's Rock and showed him the crude track to Woodford. It was a very emotional departure. They shook hands as Maas Albert promised that one day he would repay them for their kindness.

"Guidance," said Ras Jeremiah, and "Peace and love," said Ras Benjie as they separated.

Maas Albert was now on the way to Woodford and all kinds of questions were going through his mind. What had become of Ivy and the children? What of Mr. Bembridge? Who was taking care of the farm at Cherry Gardens Estate? He'd heard no news of his family or any news at all for over seven weeks. It was while going over these questions in his mind, that he entered a small banana and plantain walk owned by a man named Maas Joe.

Maas Joe was coming from his farm with a bunch of half-ripe Lakatan bananas on his head, when he saw Maas Albert. He flung the banana from his head and flattened out several young plantain shoots in his bid to escape from what he thought was Maas Albert's 'duppy'.

A wonder what the hell is going on, Maas Albert said to himself.

He entered the square in Woodford about two o'clock that Sunday afternoon. It was customary for the men in the village to gather at the village square for a drink around this time. Almost every man in the village was present. Their favorite rum talk these days was Maas Albert's death and who would take over his woman. Maas Albert appeared in his Rasta clothing and was walking towards the village bar, when the alarm was made.

"Albert duppy come, run! Albert duppy de ya!"

The men came out of the bar to look and there was Maas Albert in his white Rasta garment looking down on them. The men leaped on their donkeys, mules and horses, and they rode and ran as fast as they could in every direction. A man named Baugh wet his pants and soiled himself. One man nearly broke his neck when he attempted to jump on his donkey, the donkey ran and he came crashing to the ground. Three men jumped on one mule in another instance. The bartender ran from the bar and left it open. The ground in front of the bar was littered with rum mugs and bottles.

There was a little shop not far from the village bar where the men would stop and play dominoes. No one saw Maas Albert coming, he just went to the door and said, "Good evening gentlemen."

Luckily there was a window at the back of the shop. Four men leaped through at once; two of them fainted and one kicked through the wattle and daub wall and damaged his foot.

By this time news had gotten around that Maas Albert's duppy had come and was seen at the square in Two Threes. People locked their houses, and the children and women ran home as fast as they could. The streets were deserted as the terrified villagers peeped from their windows into the street. Men started sharpening their machetes, determined to kill the duppy. When the news reached Miss Ivy she hastily took the children and went to her neighbor's house. It was now five o'clock in the evening; Maas Albert was nearing his home and hoping to see his wife and children. There was a group of men with machetes and stones who followed at a respectable distance.

When Maas Albert got to his house he opened the little gate and entered.

"Ivy," he called, "Ivy." There was no mistaking that this was the voice of her beloved husband. Poor Miss Ivy fainted! Suzie was jubilant. "Papa, papa come!" She knew the voice of her father and would have darted out to him had they not held her.

One brave man known as Maas Natty started talking. "Albert what you doing here, go back to you grave, you nuh dead?" The men froze when Maas Albert turned and looked at them. His face was covered with hair for he had not shaved for seven weeks, his eyes looked wild and had a shiny look, and his Rasta dressing made him look indeed as one risen from the dead.

"I am not dead," he said.

"Mi seh yuh dead!" replied Maas Natty. The men were about to stone the duppy, when poor Maas Albert started crying. He cried because he remembered weeks ago when Robusta used the same words to him. He cried when he remembered how he went to death's door and how for weeks he could not move. And to make matters worse, he now came to his own village and they took him for a ghost. It was too much for Maas Albert. By this time Miss Ivy had revived and heard her husband crying. The women told her that the duppy was crying for her. She fainted again.

Maas Albert finally stopped crying and addressed the villagers in as loud and firm a voice as he could. Indeed if he didn't, they might have stoned him.

"Listen to me, oonuh stop the blasted foolishness and listen to story; I am not dead, come and touch me if you want." His stern and cutting words quieted the men and they listened. Maas Albert began his story and it lasted late into the night. He told them everything. By this time someone had reported the news to Father Paul who armed himself with his Bible and a large cross, intending to drive the duppy away. He rode his mule to Maas Albert's house. He was both thrilled and terrified at the same time as he quietly listened to the story.

But this man is not dead, he said to himself. When Maas Albert was through speaking he mustered the courage. He gingerly opened the gate and extended his right hand to Maas Albert.

"Welcome back Brother Albert." At this the villagers let out a shout; they threw their hats in the air and they jumped for joy. *Maas Albert come back and him a nuh duppy. A de real Albert*, was the chorus they chanted. They all tried to greet him and to shake his hand. *Welcome back Maas Albert, welcome back, Lord have mercy! We t'ink yuh dead, funeral keep fi yuh, but yuh alive!*

Miss Ivy ran to her husband, grabbed him and burst into bitter tears. "Albert, mi sugar dumpling, you come back, mi bununoonus! A know God wasn't gwine let mi down." When Maas Albert felt the touch of his wife as she rested her head on his chest, and when his sweet little Suzie was placed in his arms, he could not speak; the tears did the talking and all the villagers wept happily with them.

It was a night of excitement and happiness in Woodford. The villagers gathered in their numbers that Sunday night at Maas Albert's home. They just gazed upon him as though he was a great hero which indeed he was. Later he washed himself, shaved for he had not shaven in weeks, and put on fresh clothes.

Later that night when he came out to his friends in the village, he indeed looked like the real Albert Walker. Miss Ivy was jubilant, Suzie would not leave 'papa' one bit, the rest of Albert's children were overjoyed to see their father and the villagers were happy, for Albert Walker had come home.

CHAPTER 12

FATHER PAUL BRINGS GOOD NEWS TO CHERRY GARDENS ESTATE

The next day being Monday, Maas Albert thought of going at once to Cherry Gardens Estate. But by now he had grown wise. He did not want to scare Mr. Bembridge and the workers at Cherry Gardens Estate. So he asked Father Paul if he would kindly undertake the task of bearing the good news to Mr. Bembridge, to which Father Paul gladly consented.

Father Paul made good time for he left Woodford before day at 5 a.m. and by 9 a.m. he arrived at Cherry Gardens Estate. The workers were busy as usual doing their chores when father Paul rode in hastily. One could tell that he had important business. He looked regal on his black horse, clad in his black parson's suit with a broad hat and a half smile on his face. He looked more like an English beadle than a parson.

He greeted Mr. Bembridge who was reclining on his verandah with Mrs. Bembridge. After exchanging the customary pleasantries and having seated the reverend gentleman, Mr. Bembridge asked, "And what business has brought you to Cherry Gardens at this time of day Father?"

"What I'm about to say to you," replied Father Paul, "may make your hair stand on end sir, but you must hear it."

"Why man, what is it?" asked Mr. Bembridge hastily.

"Albert Walker is alive!" replied Father Paul.

One could hear a pin drop as Mr. Bembridge and his wife looked aghast at Father Paul. "What did you say Father?" he replied.

"Albert Walker is alive."

"I don't believe it; are you sure it's not his ghost?"

"So everyone thought," said Father Paul with a chuckle. "He appeared in Woodford last evening and had the entire village in consternation."

"But what happened?" asked Mr. Bembridge. "I saw him leave here myself on the stretcher with Corporal Sharpe and the burial team."

Father Paul chuckled again, then started to relate the story. When the story ended Mr. Bembridge was jubilant.

"That Sharpe must be dealt with," he said. "I knew there was something funny about him burying Albert in Jacks Hill. But thank God! Father, God be praised, Albert Walker is alive!"

Mr. Bembridge at once called a meeting with the workers on the estate and gave them the good news.

The workers could not believe their ears and naturally, there were more questions than answers. Luckily Father Paul was present to answer most of their questions. That Monday afternoon nobody wanted to work, the news of Maas Albert's ordeal and how he came back home was on everybody's lips. They all wanted to know when he would return to Cherry Gardens Estate and whether he would resume his work.

That afternoon Miss Babsy prepared a sumptuous meal of roasted beef, chicken and curried mutton. Mr. Bembridge and Father Paul ate happily and heartily, and drank the strong waters of white rum with lime. They talked and laughed together, and Babsy was the picture of health as she sprang into action.

"Maas Albert must return at once and resume his duties immediately. Tell him to take his good rest and enjoy being with his family," said Mr. Bembridge to Father Paul, "and return to work next week Monday morning early."

"Very well then," said Father Paul as they parted company.

CHAPTER 13

MAAS ALBERT AND MISS IVY IN COMPANY

Meanwhile Maas Albert had a long conversation with Miss Ivy, and she told him of the sorrow she went through when Mr. Bembridge brought the news to Woodford that Friday evening.

"Imagine Albert, I was expecting you to come home Friday and prepared your usual cock soup only to get news that you died of cholera!"

She told him of the nine-night, the funeral service, and how the whole village came out in support of him. Maas Albert listened with much satisfaction, laughing now and then and asking odd questions about who said what, and this and that.

Miss Ivy continued, "Imagine Maas White him come a put question to me, bout marriage."

"What!" said Maas Albert, "you mean that old drunkard?"

"Never mind mi love," said Miss Ivy, "everybody think say you dead, so when puss gone rat nuh tek ova!"

Maas Albert roared with laughter. "Yes, nuh mi a de dead puss!" He roared with laughter again.

Just to hear his laughter again, just to have her dear husband at home again, felt so good. Miss Ivy laughed and cried at the same time. Then she said, "I couldn't see myself marrying any other man but you; that's why I was making preparations to leave Woodford and start a life in Kingston or travel to England."

"Live in Kingston! Travel to England? And where would you get that money Ivy?"

Miss Ivy rested her hand on his shoulders while he sat in his favorite chair and told him, "Your boss Mr. Bembridge gave me two hundred pounds as a reward for your service of twenty-three years working at Cherry Gardens Estate."

"Two hundred pounds Ivy, you mean two hundred pounds! So much money? Where is it?"

"Calm yourself," said Miss Ivy, "I deposited one hundred and ninety-seven pounds in the bank at King Street and I used the rest for your funeral."

"But Ivy, we have to return it, for mi no dead."

"Is the same thing on my mind," said Miss Ivy. "Imagine, death bring riches and life brings poverty."

"For the first time mi feel like fi dead again," said Maas Albert, with a laugh.

"Foolishness," said Miss Ivy. "Better to have life and live in poverty, than to have death with riches."

"Albert!" Miss Ivy continued. "You will never know what I went through. Yes, I was glad for the money but I will gladly give it back to Bembridge because you came home. No amount of money can replace you."

They hugged each other.

CHAPTER 14

PREPARATIONS TO RETURN TO WORK

Father Paul visited Maas Albert Tuesday morning and gave a detailed report of his visit with Mr. Bembridge. Maas Albert was to return to work the next Monday, and resume his job as manager at Cherry Gardens Estate. Mr. Bembridge had asked Jones, one of his men, to assume the position as manager but since learning of Maas Albert's return, he had relinquished the temporary appointment.

Miss Ivy made a fresh flour-bag shirt for him, and she took out a brand new pants she had in storage and ironed it. The boys polished their father's boots until they could see their faces in it. His work bag, his tools, his machete and wallet, all were brought back to his house by Mr. Bembridge. His faithful mule Lyder was shod with brand new horse shoes and other accessories, even his hair was combed as Maas Albert made preparation for going back to work.

Early the following Monday morning Maas Albert was on his way to Cherry Gardens Estate. He wore a new English hat, he had on his brand new clean white flour-bag shirt, nice black boots and black Sandburg pants, his face was radiant from hours of rest, and he looked the picture of health. Lyder his mule was equally happy to have his master back and trotted happily along as they made their way through Norbrook into Constant Spring.

Before reaching Congo Town he paused and looked across the valleys from Peter's Rock to Jacks Hill. He could see a faint outline of the foot track in Jacks Hill and the treacherous precipice from which he slid to escape being buried alive. He could not believe his eyes.

From the look of things he estimated that he had slid at least four or five hundred feet from Jacks Hill straight down into Norbrook. *This was nothing short of a miracle,* he said to himself. He vowed to visit the two Rasta men someday and return the kindness they had showed to him. He was now crossing the Constant Spring river and would soon be on the main road to Cherry Gardens Estate.

He had travelled on this road countless times, but this Monday morning he sensed a new appreciation for life and the pleasure of seeing his stomping ground again. As he entered Cherry Gardens Estate, his heart beat a little faster than usual, as all kinds of thoughts arose in his mind. He was as one risen from the dead, they had witnessed his body being carried out of the estate, most of the workers including those whom he supervised had attended his funeral service, and would Mr. Bembridge demand the return of the two hundred pounds he gave to Miss Ivy?

He arrived at the great house at about 8:15 a.m. to find the entire staff assembled on the verandah. As he rode slowly towards them, the workers clapped and shouted, "Welcome back Maas Albert! Welcome back!"

Miss Babsy and Mrs. Bembridge were in tears as Maas Albert dismounted Lyder and walked towards them. Mr. Bembridge had watery eyes as he walked towards Maas Albert with his hands outstretched. Poor Maas Albert broke down as Mr. Bembridge shook his hands and slapped him on the back. The men had teary eyes, the women openly wept tears of joy as Maas Albert stood among them. Hat in hand, he just stood there weeping.

When he had composed himself he said between sobs, "Sir, I didn't know that the Almighty would allow me to walk these grounds again, to shake your hand, and to see the workers of Cherry Gardens Estate. Thank you for your prayers and for the support you gave to my wife and children while I was presumed dead. I also thank you sir, for accepting me again as your manager."

Mr. Bembridge replied, "Don't mention it Albert, it is enough just to have you back, I welcome you back to Cherry Gardens Estate, not just as a manager but as a friend."

CHAPTER 15

TO SEE SUPERINTENDENT STARKEY

After the workers were dispatched to their various chores Mr. Bembridge had a long talk with Maas Albert. Maas Albert indeed gave his own account of his ordeal. He told him that when he left on the stretcher that Thursday evening he wasn't dead, but was unconscious due to the high fever and pain. When they carried him outside, the cool breeze slowed the fever and by the time he reached Jacks Hill, the fever had gone down enough wherein he regained a little consciousness. He heard the men talking about his burial and started protesting, but Corporal Sharpe would have none of it. That was when he rolled from the stretcher and slid more than three hundred feet down the precipice. Mr. Bembridge listened intently and when

Maas Albert was through, he called for the four men who had accompanied Corporal Sharpe to bury Maas Albert. Two of the men smelled the rat and opted to leave Cherry Gardens Estate immediately. The other two presented themselves like penitent souls before Mr. Bembridge, who went straight to the point.

"Did you not report to me some weeks ago that you buried this man in Jacks Hill?"

"Yes sar but Robusta say him dead."

"Did you bury him?" asked Mr. Bembridge.

"No sar him bury himself, and Robusta say him dead."

"Robusta say him dead! Look at this man, does he look like a dead man?"

"No sar, but Robusta say him dead."

"You lying brutes, how much did he pay you for telling such an egregious lie?"

"Ten shillings sar."

Mr. Bembridge slapped his boots with his cane.

"What should I do with these men Albert?"

"A beg you give them a chance sar."

"What!" said Mr. Bembridge.

"Give them a chance," said Maas Albert. "Sir, Robusta is to be blamed, that man would turn a saint into the devil if he got the chance."

"I suppose you are right," said Mr. Bembridge. He dismissed the men with a stern warning, then he and Maas Albert mounted two horses and headed for Half Way Tree to the police station to see Superintendent Starkey.

Superintendent Starkey received them heartily for while he was aware of Maas Albert's death, he had not yet learnt of his so called resurrection. When the story was outlined to him he became white with rage and summoned Robusta immediately.

Meanwhile, Robusta was busy in the barracks doing what he liked best, slapping the prisoners around with his tamarind switch. He was the dread and terror of the lock-up. When he got the message from Superintendent Starkey he rudely asked, "A wonder what dat white man want wid me now?" Of late he and Superintendent Starkey had not been on good terms. He was known to voice openly that the white man didn't know what he was doing, and that he, Robusta, could do a better job. Starkey may have used this opportunity to get back at Corporal Sharpe.

Maas Albert was asked to step out of Superintendent Starkey's office briefly, while Corporal Sharpe was ushered in. "What you want wid me now sah?" he asked roughly.

"Mr. Walker would you come in now?"

Maas Albert stepped from within the side room and presented himself squarely before Robusta.

Robusta attempted to jump through the window. Luckily he was grabbed by Mr. Bembridge and Superintendent Starkey, otherwise he would have jumped two stories high and hurt himself. When he had composed himself, Superintendent Starkey asked him, "Do you know this man?"

"This is a dead man, mi bury him mi self!"

"Don't form the fool," said Superintendent Starkey, "does he look like a dead man?"

Still belligerent, Corporal Sharpe continued, "Boss I don't know how this duppy come to be here, all I know is that a buried him in Jacks Hill."

"You didn't bury me, you liar!" said Maas Albert, "indeed you would have buried me alive if I didn't roll myself from the stretcher that Thursday night. You cruel monster! You thought I was dead, but the Lord rescued me and now I stand before you to condemn you!"

"Condemn who?" asked Corporal Sharpe.

"You," said Superintendent Starkey, who now took over the conversation. "You have been unfaithful to your trust, you have accepted money for a job you didn't do, and you have lied to myself and Mr. Bembridge, and encouraged Mr. Bembridge's men to lie under the circumstances!"

There was a long pause as the three men stared in disgust at Robusta. Then he spoke, "Boss you said I have been unfaithful to my trust, you are right, I should have buried him in Jacks Hill, but I can still bury him now if you want!"

"Drat!" Superintendent Starkey slapped his staff so hard on his desk, the room vibrated. "You're already in enough trouble, yet you insist on being a baboon! Leave this room sir, go home and don't return to work until you hear from me!"

Robusta took his hat, his switch and whatever little dignity he had left and went home. He was later transferred to the Spanish Town police station.

CHAPTER 16

A SLOW AND PLEASANT RIDE TO CHERRY GARDENS ESTATE

Maas Albert and Mr. Bembridge left the Half Way Tree police station about one o'clock that afternoon. The sun was not as hot as the sky was overcast with light cumulus clouds which covered the parishes of Kingston and St. Andrew. They rode slowly. Mr. Bembridge had a smile of satisfaction on his face, then he asked, "I wonder what Dr. Benjamin will say when he learns of this affair?"

Maas Albert had a question of his own which he wanted to ask Mr. Bembridge. And this was the opportune time.

"Sir," he said. "While I was presumed dead my wife Ivy told me that you gave her two hundred pounds as payment for my services at Cherry Gardens."

"What of it?" said Mr. Bembridge.

"Well," said Maas Albert, "I was wondering if I should not pay back the dead money."

Mr. Bembridge roared with laughter, he could not contain himself. He just laughed and laughed. When he was through, he said, "Maas Albert your resurrection has brought me nothing but joy. You may keep the money, and by the way I will be leaving for England next month. In my absence I leave you in full charge of Cherry Gardens until my return in six months' time."

"Thank you sir," Maas Albert replied as they rode through the gate which led to Cherry Gardens. Maas Albert remained as manager of Cherry Gardens Estate, his wife Miss Ivy much affected by the turn of events, moved unto Cherry Gardens Estate with her husband. They were allowed to live in one of the smaller houses on the estate and returned together on weekends to Woodford.

Mr. Bembridge continued to prosper as owner of Cherry Gardens Estate until his death in 1904. The story of Maas Albert Walker's death, burial and resurrection was still told to this day.

Walk good.

www.ingramcontent.com/pod-product-compliance
Lightning Source LLC
Chambersburg PA
CBHW050833180626
46814CB00004B/1603